S0-ASO-908

HOW TO HELP
A GUIDE TO
Giving
Back

WAYS TO HELP
AFTER A NATURAL
DISASTER

Laya Saul

Mitchell Lane
PUBLISHERS

P.O. Box 196
Hockessin, DE 19707
www.mitchelllane.com

PUBLISHERS

Ways to Help After a Natural Disaster
Ways to Help Children With Disabilities
Ways to Help Chronically Ill Children
Ways to Help Disadvantaged Youth
Ways to Help in Your Community
Ways to Help the Elderly
Volunteering in Your School
Celebrities Giving Back

Copyright © 2011 by Mitchell Lane Publishers

All rights reserved. No part of this book may be reproduced without written permission from the publisher. Printed and bound in the United States of America.

PUBLISHER'S NOTE: The facts on which the story in this book is based have been thoroughly researched. Documentation of such research can be found on page 45. While every possible effort has been made to ensure accuracy, the publisher will not assume liability for damages caused by inaccuracies in the data, and makes no warranty on the accuracy of the information contained herein.

Library of Congress
Cataloging-in-Publication Data

Saul, Laya.
  Ways to help after a natural disaster / by Laya Saul.
      p. cm. — (How to help : a guide to giving back)
  Includes bibliographical references and index.
  ISBN 978-1-58415-917-9 (library bound)
  1. Disaster relief—Juvenile literature. 2. Voluntarism—Juvenile literature. I. Title.
  HV553.S28 2011
  363.34'8—dc22
                                              2010006538

Printing   1   2   3   4   5   6   7   8   9

                                              PLB

CONTENTS

Introduction 4

Chapter One
Teaching Preparedness 7

Chapter Two
Connecting in an Emergency 11

Chapter Three
Volunteer Your Time or Skills 15

Chapter Four
Giving Emotional Support to Other Kids 18

Chapter Five
Organizing Child Care While Adults Rebuild 21

Chapter Six
Blood Drive 24

Chapter Seven
Food and Clothing Drives 26

Chapter Eight
Fund-raising for Charities 29

Chapter Nine
Replanting 33

Chapter Ten
Grassroots 35

Resources 38

Further Reading 45

Books 45

Works Consulted 45

On the Internet 45

Index 47

Introduction

Have you ever lost something you really did not want to lose? Maybe you lost a wallet with money in it, or a favorite piece of jewelry, or maybe something even more valuable. You can imagine how sad it would feel for someone to lose a whole house with everything he or she owns: clothing, photos, furniture, perhaps a pet, or maybe, saddest of all, a loved one. Losses like these are some of the devastating results of natural disasters.

A natural disaster is any type of storm or natural hazard that causes environmental destruction, financial loss, and often the loss of life. Heavy rains that bring flooding or mudslides, wildfires, earthquakes, blizzards, and hurricanes are all types of natural disasters. Terrorism and contamination by hazardous materials are also classified as natural disasters, even though humans cause them. According to the Federal Emergency Management Agency (FEMA), millions of Americans are affected by natural disasters each year.

Even in times of grief and loss, there is a chance to help rebuild in positive ways. After a big loss, people may feel

completely alone; but when good people step forward to come together, to lend a hand and a smile, hope shines through and brings healing to the darkest places.

That's what this book is about: sharing ideas for things you can do to help people and communities repair and heal after a natural disaster. Some of the ideas are simple and easy to do; others require more planning and organization. Some you can do on your own, and some you can do with your parents or friends. Please feel free to use the ideas in this book just the way they are or to change them in ways that best use your talents and match the situation you are facing. The main thing is that you share your heart through the actions you take—that alone will help people feel better. Every small action can truly make a big difference to comfort people or even save lives.

Always make sure you have your parents' permission and supervision to work on any of these ideas. If you want to help younger kids, make sure you have the permission of the children's parents or guardians as well.

A boy ties off a sandbag as he and his community in Illinois prepare for a flood. After heavy rains swelled a nearby river, the community began preparing to protect their town from the rising waters. Kids at any age can find even small ways to help. Working as part of a team rebuilds the community.

Teaching Preparedness

Learn to make an emergency preparedness kit.

Both the Federal Emergency Management Agency (FEMA) and the American Red Cross (ARC) agree that every home should be prepared for a natural disaster with an emergency preparedness kit. The kit should include basic supplies and should be stored in a designated place in your home. That means once your kit is put together, your family decides the best place to keep it in your home (a cool place that is easy to get to), and everyone knows it's there. You can help your family prepare a kit, and then teach others how they can prepare one for their families. Smaller kits for cars or offices are also a good idea.

While some disasters are seasonal, like blizzards in winter, other disasters, such as earthquakes, can happen at any time and without warning. Be prepared. When disaster strikes, time is a luxury you may not have.

Make a Preparedness Kit

Each region has its own kind of possible natural disaster, and each disaster might need different supplies. For example, where there are earthquakes, a kit might include heavy

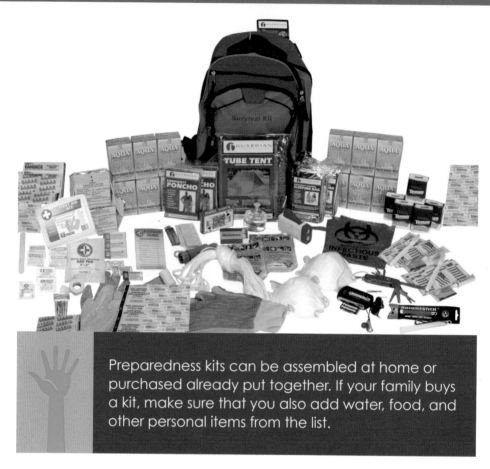

Preparedness kits can be assembled at home or purchased already put together. If your family buys a kit, make sure that you also add water, food, and other personal items from the list.

boots for walking through a home that has a lot of broken glass. People in a region that experiences blizzards will want to put extra blankets in their kits. However, there are some basic items that every kit should have.

Make a list of items for you and your family to include in a preparedness kit. Use the basic supply list on page 9, then add items for disasters that are specific to your region of the country. Several web sites that list these items can be found on page 45.

In the Event of Evacuation

A preparedness kit should be in one or two containers that can be easily moved if your family has to evacuate. Duffel

BASIC SUPPLY KIT FOR A NATURAL DISASTER

- One gallon of drinking water per day, per person—a three-day supply

- Three-day supply of food for each person in the home—include food that will not spoil and that does not need to be cooked: canned goods (with manual opener); dried meats and fruit; nuts or peanut butter; crackers; health bars; and infant formula

- Spare clothing: if there are children, the clothing for them should be switched out as they grow. One idea is to put in clothes that are the next size up, and when they grow into that size, switch them

- Bedding: extra blankets for colder areas

- First aid kit with manual

- Sanitation and medical supplies: this includes any prescription medicines people in the family take and general over-the-counter products that someone might need; also diapers, feminine hygiene products, toilet paper, wet wipes, trash bags

- Flashlight and batteries: the batteries should be kept separately to keep them fresh; extra batteries

- Portable radio: the batteries should be kept separate to keep them fresh; extra batteries

- Pet supplies: a dish, food, leash, blanket

- Whistle (to signal for help)

- Waterproof matches

- Extra: comfort items, such as a deck of cards, picture books, comic books, or prayer books

- A checklist, instructions, and the tools you would need for turning off the gas, electricity, and water supply

- A list of emergency contacts (see chapter 2)

- Cash in small denominations (power may be out at ATMs and cash registers)

Extra Tip: Put a note at the bottom of the list to remind people to stay calm and kind during times of emergency.

bags, storage containers, or small, clean garbage cans with lids work well. A short list taped to the outside of the kit can serve as a reminder to grab cell phones with chargers, a child's favorite stuffed animal, refrigerated medicines, or, if there's time and room, family photos.

Spread the Word

Once you have made your list and gathered supplies for your family, you can make copies of your list and hand them out. On the back of the list, you could also put emergency phone numbers for your area. (See chapter 2 to find out how to put together a list of phone numbers.)

Where would you give out copies of a list like this? Think of creative ways you can reach your neighbors. You could take the list door to door (if you do, ask **an adult** to accompany you, and do not enter homes of people you do not know). You could also ask permission from a local store to set up an information table for customers. The store might even sponsor a project like this. Talk to someone at the service desk, and find out who would be the best person to talk to about your idea. Some businesses might be happy to make or pay for the copies of the list you want to pass out. If they do, they might want their names on the flyer too.

A campaign in your school is a good way to get the word out to a lot of families. Make a presentation to your class about what people should have in their kits at home and in the car. Ask the students who see your presentation to spread the word in their neighborhoods. After your presentation, you can pass out extra lists for students to take home.

Extra Tip: Remind your parents to always keep at least a quarter tank of gas in the car—or a full tank if there's a chance you'll have to evacuate. If you have to leave an area immediately, gas may not be available. You don't want to run out of gas before you have reached safety.

Chapter **2**

Connecting in an Emergency

Make a list of all important phone numbers. Have a plan.

It is important to keep a list of emergency phone numbers handy in a home kit. Many phone books list emergency numbers at the front. You can also find phone numbers online for hospitals, police departments, utilities, and other places. You can photocopy the list on page 12 to get started.

In the event that phone lines are down, have a plan of where to meet your family. Also, designate an out-of-town relative everyone can call to keep in touch. Since local phone lines may be tied up, it could actually be easier to call out of state than to call locally. That person can report to others when they call in.

Once you have put your list together, show it to a few people you respect to see if they would add any other service numbers important to your area.

Fill out a copy for yourself, but on the copies you want to pass out, leave the personal numbers blank for others to fill in. The first part of the list with all the family contact information is a great thing for every family member to carry in a backpack or notebook, purse, briefcase, or glove compartment of the car. It's a good idea to program all

EMERGENCY PHONE NUMBERS

People Connections
Mom's cell:
Work:

Dad's cell:
Work:

Kids' cell:

Neighbors:

Local relatives:

Out-of-town contact #1 (each family member should call if the family is split up):

Out-of-town contact #2:

Emergency Numbers
911 (This number works in most U.S. areas; be sure to fill in the other local numbers just in case.)

Fire department:

Police:

Ambulance:

Utilities
Electric company:

Gas company:

Water company:

Emergency Organizations
Red Cross:

FEMA:

Local Schools (and schools where kids in the family learn)
Elementary:

Junior high:

High:

Local Grocery Stores

Medical
Poison Control: 1-800-222-1222

Hospitals:

Ambulance:
(This is listed twice on purpose so that even under stress it will be found)

Urgent Care:
(List known allergies or medical conditions of each family member here)

Doctors' Offices
Family doctor:

Pediatrician:

Pharmacy:

Veterinarian:

numbers into a cell phone, but it's also a good idea to have the numbers printed on paper in case the cell phone is lost or the battery loses its charge.

Have a Plan

Every family should have a plan for what to do in an emergency at the house. For example, to prepare for a house fire, plan how to escape from each room, and make it clear where to meet outside the house. It is best to go to a neighbor's house where someone can call the fire department. However, if there are no neighbors close by, plan to meet at a particular location that would be a safe distance from the house—perhaps at the end of the driveway, if it's long enough. Once you are out of the house, stay out. Discuss fire safety and escape plans with your family every month, and change the batteries in smoke detectors whenever you change the clocks for Daylight Savings Time.

For other emergencies, such as a hurricane or tornado, it may be safer to stay inside the house than to leave it. Before a hurricane or tornado, decide where you will gather: in a room in the basement—one with no windows—or in the center of the house. In an earthquake, sit under a heavy table, away from glass that could shatter or objects that could fall. If you are expecting a storm that may knock out

Extra Tip: If you go online you can sign up for a free blog to list resources for your community. If you want to make a blog, try using the name "preparedinyourtown" and substitute the name of your city or town. For example, if you live in Hayward, your blog name could be preparedinhayward. You can build your blog on online sites such as blogger.com, wordpress.com, and blog.com. Once you get your blog up, be sure to let all your friends and schoolmates know about it through e-mail or through any social networking sites you already use (such as Twitter or Facebook).

the power, fill a bathtub with water for use after the disaster. (Keep the door closed to protect small children.)

Since the kinds of disasters that strike are different in different places, you should learn what the hazards are in your state and be prepared with a plan. For example, some states may have days of warning before a flood or hurricane, giving people time to evacuate. Other disasters may arrive without warning.

After a disaster, your home may not be livable. Mark Benthien, Director of Education and Outreach of the Southern California Earthquake Center, advises people to camp in their yards if possible, since shelters could be crowded. In a flood, it is not advisable to walk or swim in deep water—and people should never drive through floodwater. If the water is high, go to the roof of a building and wait for rescue.

Your local radio station should broadcast instructions during a time of emergency through the Emergency Alert System (EAS). The U.S. government is also preparing to implement the Integrated Public Alert and Warning System (IPAWS), which will expand the EAS. Be sure to tune in to your radio or any other available communication device so that you will know what is happening, where you can go, and what you should do.

The community—you and the people around you—are called "first response" because local people are the first ones who will be able to respond in an emergency. While waiting for rescue, you'll have to rely on each other's skills. If anyone is in critical condition, someone may need to go for help if a call won't go through to rescuers.

Chapter 3

Volunteer Your Time or Skills

Help with cleaning up and taking care of seniors and animals.

In the aftermath of a disaster, there will certainly be a lot to do in the community. Call centers and shelters may need your help. Try calling a local branch of the Red Cross to see if you can volunteer. When calling the police department about volunteer work, be sure you call the local office number; 911 is *for emergency use only*.

Cleaning Up

Floods and tornadoes can leave a huge mess. Some messes are so extreme that professionals must be hired because of the danger involved in the cleanup. Others just require cleanup of broken items in the home or things that got tossed around in the yard or street. Decide on the area you want to help clean. You don't have to clean the whole town or street. Cleaning up even a little bit makes a difference. If you get a group of friends or family members to work together, you can make the time go by in a fun way. Be sure that you have the supplies you need before going out to clean up:

Proper shoes: sturdy, closed-toe, with a thick sole
Work gloves, such as heavy gardening gloves or heavy
    rubber gloves
Heavy trash bags or trash cans for debris

Caring for Seniors

If you have family members or neighbors who are seniors, they may be feeling very afraid or alone. Spending time with them, helping them clean up their houses or yards, making sure they have food, or just keeping them company is a wonderful use of your time. Reading to a senior or playing a game, doing puzzles together, or listening to their stories about a different generation is a kindness that has no measure.

Caring for Animals

If you love animals, volunteering at your local animal shelter can be a fun way to spread your compassion. Pets get separated from their owners for any number of reasons, and shelters that are set up to take care of people will not allow pets. The work to take care of animals is enormous, and the people who work at shelters don't always have the time to devote to each pet, even when there is not a disaster situation. If you have to be a minimum age to help at an animal shelter, you might be able to work if a parent or older sibling comes with you. Call ahead to find out.

Jobs that might need your efforts:
Taking puppies or dogs to the exercise yard
Feeding animals
Cleaning up after animals (this may not be the most fun
    job, but it is a really important one!)
Petting and giving animals attention
Phone calls to owners to tell them that their pets have
    been found

A volunteer looks after two puppies at a rescue center that was set up in Louisiana after Hurricane Katrina. Workers and volunteers from the Society for Prevention of Cruelty to Animals (SPCA) and Humane Society had the animals washed, treated for disease, and photographed so that they could be identified and retrieved by their owners.

Please be careful about handling animals. Accept the guidance and directions of the workers at the shelter. They are around the animals all the time and know how to be with them, which ones you should not handle, and so on. Each animal shelter has its own system for getting things done. You just have to be flexible.

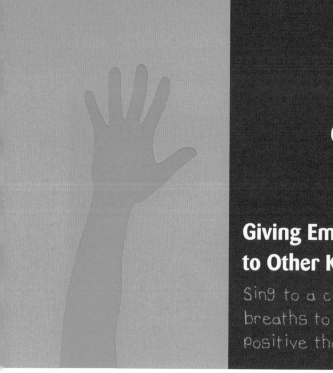

Chapter 4

Giving Emotional Support to Other Kids

Sing to a child, take deep breaths to relax, and think positive thoughts.

After a natural disaster, some kids might feel very frightened. While adults are running around tending to emergency situations, some children may wind up on the sidelines, scared and crying. Just being with a child your age and talking makes the difference between feeling alone and feeling cared for. For a smaller child, a warm hug, reading a storybook, or even singing a song can help. No one likes to feel alone in a scary situation, so any attention you give to someone who needs it can go a long way.

There are things you can do with children who feel stressed from the emotions and fears that result from a natural disaster. If you are near or taking care of children after a trauma, never force them to do something (unless their direct safety is involved); always invite them gently. You can do these things for yourself too!

The Universal Comfort of a Song
Often a young child will feel comforted by a song sung softly. Think of gentle songs with positive words. Maybe you know some songs from summer camp. You can sing songs that you

Caring for babies and younger children can have a real impact on lessening trauma and lifting spirits. It can give parents a chance to do other tasks or get some needed rest. The gift of sharing yourself in these ways will bring you satisfaction for a lifetime!

learned where your family worships. If you can't think of something on the spur of the moment, you can make up a song. Just start humming anything, and if you want to, you can make up some simple words that are comforting.

Deep-Breathing Techniques to Relax

Taking a simple deep breath is a great technique for helping anyone to relax (including you!). In fact, don't save this one for an emergency; you can use it before bed or any other time you or one of your friends feels stressed. You can practice and encourage this easy technique. Here's how:

Sitting with your back straight, start by being aware of your breath coming in and out. Take a deep breath in and let it out with a whoosh. Do this a few times, and each time you let your breath go, imagine any fear or upsetting thing leaving your body and floating up to the sky to be healed.

When you start to feel more relaxed, take a deep breath and imagine the breath going into your belly, then filling into your middle, then your chest. As you let the breath out, sink your chest, middle, and belly so that all the air goes out. Just a few breaths like this will do wonders. Then just breathe naturally again.

Positive Self-Talk

Sometimes children just need to be encouraged. Tell them how strong they are, how good they are, or that they are not alone. Letting a child know that it is natural to feel afraid is fine too. Never try to make children get over their tears by telling them they are acting like a baby. It could backfire and make them feel worse. The way to talk with a frightened child is by using words of love and encouragement:

"I know how scary this must have been for you. You are okay now."

"You are so brave! I'm very proud of you!"

"You are all right now. You are not alone. I'm right here."

Chapter 5

Organizing Child Care While Adults Rebuild

Make other kids feel safe. Read to them, tell them stories, organize projects, and play games with them.

If something happens in a community that requires a longer time for organizing safety or rebuilding after damage, it's a wonderful service to help with younger kids. Shelters may be set up by rescue organizations, or you might be able to help just in your own neighborhood. Here are some ideas of things you can do if you spend time watching younger kids.

Organize Art Projects

Some simple paper and crayons, paints, or pencils are enough to let children express themselves; just let them go with their ideas. This is the place to praise each child who participates. It's not about technique; it's about feeling better and expressing emotions.

If your library is up and running, you could also check out books on guided art activities. There are dozens of simple art

Extra Tip: As you do projects for young kids, invite a parent to come and be with the child. It could be very healing and a relief for a parent to have a planned activity to go to.

projects you can do with kids, from papier-mâché to puppets.

Storytelling

Look in your library or maybe on your own bookshelf for books with great stories you can read to children. Choose stories according to the age of the kids you'll read to, but be flexible because often kids who are already reading on their own still enjoy a good picturebook! Your librarian can help you pick great books. Try to choose stories where the main characters triumph. Have fun when you read out loud. Do different voices for the characters. It's okay to be goofy around kids; it's fun for them, and you may even discover some hidden talents of your own!

Basic Games You Can Play with Kids
Red Light/Green Light
Freeze Tag
Duck, Duck, Goose
Simon Says
Telephone

Snack Time

If you're working with kids, try to have snacks and drinks on hand. Kids have little stomachs and get hungry every couple of hours. Healthy snacks include crackers, carrot sticks, fruits, and nuts. Make sure you talk with each child's parents to check for special dietary needs. Some kids have severe allergies, and you'll have to avoid foods that can trigger them.

Extra Tip: Make sure you have the contact information for the parents of any child you are baby-sitting!

The more fun and dramatic you are with your reading, the more the kids will be engaged. Different or funny voices, and sometimes making your voice louder and softer, will make for a good time with books. If you read before the children's naptime, use a very soft, quiet voice to calm everyone down.

Stress Relief

Review the ideas in chapter 4 if a child still feels frightened or upset.

Chapter 6

Blood Drive

Help organize a blood drive. Blood donations can help save lives.

In 1989, Flight 232, on its way from Denver to Chicago, lost control. It was a dramatic and frightening situation as the brave pilot and crew of that plane maneuvered to land on an airstrip in the middle of cornfields. (Their story was even made into a movie.) The disaster was covered by the news. Local residents responded by lining up around the block to donate blood in case there were injured survivors, and a fast-food restaurant brought them snacks to eat. The plane made a crash landing and the injured were brought to area hospitals, which were prepared to receive them.

When people are injured, the need for blood to help them survive is high. Immediately after a disaster, you may be able to donate blood at the nearest medical center. However, you don't need to wait for a disaster to give.

In most states, a blood donor needs to be 17 years or older. Some states will allow someone who is 16 to donate with parental permission. Even if you are not old enough to donate blood, you are old enough to make a difference by helping others donate. That makes you a link in saving lives. That's a big deal.

Helping to organize a blood drive is truly the gift of life. One person's donation can save up to three lives because the blood can be divided into its different components, or parts. A blood drive can be done in two ways: One is to organize the event to take place at a high school or college, at some place of work, or maybe even a mall, and then let the Red Cross or another blood-collecting organization do the rest. The other simple way to get people to donate is to ask them. Most Americans are able to donate blood, yet most do not—simply because they have never been asked!

One young man was afraid to give blood because he thought it would hurt, but he found out the whole process was fast and not painful. And donating blood doesn't take that long, either—about an hour.

If you decide you want to organize a blood drive, you'll need to make some decisions:

Which organization will you work with? The Red Cross is a great place to start, but there are other centers that collect blood as well.

When do you want to have the blood drive? Set a date and a time.

Let people know about it and *invite* people to come to donate blood. All donation sites provide juice and cookies for donors. Save lives and get free snacks—what could be better?

You can go online (http://www.givelife2.org/sponsor/checklist. asp) and get a checklist from the Red Cross, complete from setting goals to booking appointments.

Chapter 7

Food and Clothing Drives

Find an organization that can distribute food and clothes, and make flyers about what to do.

If homes are destroyed or if people are not able to get to their homes because of a natural disaster, they will need food and clothing until they can get home again. Food and clothing drives are essential steps in disaster relief. Before you begin collecting, though, make sure you know where you will bring the items, that what you collect is needed, and that the organization you bring them to has a way to distribute them. Find charities in the phone book or online and contact a representative to make sure you are on track with your project.

Food

Food that you collect for a drive should be nonperishable; that means the food won't go bad quickly and doesn't need a refrigerator. Nonperishable items have been dried or canned and mostly don't need to be cooked in order to be eaten. If you're hosting a food drive, ask for things like these:

Canned goods: Vegetables, fruit, fish, meat, pasta meals (think of the kinds of food you'd like to get)

Dry goods: Crackers, cookies, cereal, tea, coffee
Jars: Peanut butter, jelly, baby food

Clothing

It is hard for some people to accept gifts. No one likes to feel like they need charity. And the people you'll be collecting for have just been through some very hard times! Giving to others in a way that helps them keep their dignity is the kindest type of giving. Keeping that in mind, when you ask people to donate clothing, ask them for the following:

Clothing that is in good repair. That means it does not have holes, rips, or stains.
Clothing and bedding that are clean.
Extras like clean, cute stuffed animals. These will probably find arms that will be happy to hold them.
If the weather is cold, blankets, coats, sweaters, and scarves will go a long way in helping to keep people warm.

How to Hold a Clothing or Food Drive

Find out where you should bring the donations you gather. Look for an organization that can distribute food or clothes to the disaster area. Local religious or civics groups are a source for organizing or distributing clothing (for example: churches, scouting groups, Red Cross, Lions Club, Salvation Army). You can find them in your local phone book or online, or ask other people in your community for ideas. Ask what kinds of things are most needed—it could be bedding or jackets or food.

Make a flyer you can pass out in your neighborhood, school, or workplace. You can handwrite a flyer or get a bit fancier and print one from your computer. Be sure to include the following information:

It is very important that you make sure whatever you collect is needed! Before you begin, know what to collect and where to deliver it.

what you are collecting (for example: clean clothes in good repair)

when you will come back to collect

where people should leave their donations for pickup, or where they can drop them off

who will be distributing the donated items, and who will receive them

why these donations are needed

Take your flyer to a copy shop for copies (a local business might even donate the flyers if you ask). Hand out the flyers, but be sure you keep track of where you give them out so that you can be sure to go back to collect.

If you want to, you can even call or e-mail your local newspaper, radio, or TV station. They make public service announcements to help promote charity events such as food or clothing drives. Be prepared with a copy of your flyer so that you can answer questions.

Chapter 8

Fund-raising for Charities

Help organize fund-raisers to make money, such as a car wash, lemonade stand, or bake sale. Set up a donation table.

There are charities all around the country that are ready to spring into action in case of an emergency. The one thing they always need is money, whether for food, water, medical supplies, or rebuilding. Fund-raising is best done for a specific organization that you know is trustworthy. It could be a national organization such as Save the Children or a local group.

Before you begin, make sure you know exactly which charity will receive the money you raise. It is smart to ask adults you know for ideas about which charity will best serve the needs of the cause you want to help. Choosing an organization that is established with a good reputation is important. Contact a representative of the charity you'd like to support. You can look in the phone book or online for a phone number or e-mail address. Ask if they have guidelines you'll need to follow in raising funds. You'll want to send a check, not cash, to the organization, so be sure you ask the person how checks should be made out and how to spell the name of the charity.

After Hurricane Katrina devastated New Orleans in 2005, kids all around the country put up lemonade stands to raise money and help the people who were left homeless. This chapter has some other ideas for raising money to help. No matter how you raise the funds for your charity, be sure to thank everyone who donates money or time.

Running or Swimming Laps

Get people you know to sponsor you for a set amount of money per lap you run or swim. You can ask people to pledge whatever amount they feel comfortable with. It's a good idea to tell people what your goal is. For example, if you are going to swim twenty laps, and they sponsor you for a dollar a lap, they know what they'll be in for. After you do the swim or run, you'll need to go back to collect the pledges. This is something that can be organized for a whole scouting troop, club, or school class.

What you'll need:
Paper with space for names, phone numbers, addresses, and amounts pledged
Envelopes to collect the money
Pens
A place to run or swim—be sure the date you want is available

Setting Up a Donation Table

If you want to set up a donation table, be sure to display a sign that tells people what you are doing and for what cause. When a natural disaster is local, you can just display the name of the cause without explaining it. If you want to help a more distant disaster, though, you may need to tell people what happened. Be prepared to tell them the name of the organization for which you are collecting.

When Johnny Wilson was nine, he swam from Alcatraz Island to Aquatic Park in San Francisco. He made the 1.4-mile swim in one hour and eight minutes. His efforts raised about $30,000 for Hurricane Katrina relief.

It helps people to be more generous if they know what their money will buy. For example, you can tell them: "Every ten dollars buys a first aid kit" or "Every fifteen dollars buys a week of fresh water" and so on, according to whatever the charity you're collecting for says. (Be sure you get the true numbers from the organization you're working for.) Keep handy the name and phone number of your contact person at the organization in case someone wants to speak directly with him or her.

In addition to your parents' permission, you *must* have the permission of the store manager at any location where you want to set up a table.

Students in a Tennessee school collect coins for a tsunami disaster in Asia. Small change adds up to dollars that bring relief to damaged areas.

Bake Sale

If you want to hold a bake sale, ask people who like to bake to prepare cookies, cupcakes, breads, or other baked goods. Then you and your friends can sell them at a church or club event. Set up a table, and decide how much you want to charge per item. Post the prices, and put up a sign saying where the money will be donated. You can also sell drinks—bottled water or soda that you buy in bulk or on sale, or even cups of coffee (be sure to provide sugar, cream, and stir sticks). Again, you'll need the permission of the manager or coordinator of the location you would like to use before you begin this project.

Chapter 9

Replanting

Find out what can be grown in the area and help plant new trees, shrubs, and flowers.

Plants and trees have all kinds of "green" benefits. They hold the soil to prevent mudslides, they provide oxygen that humans and our animal buddies need, they are home to countless species of animals and insects, and they add beauty to our surroundings. If you would like to use your talents and energy replanting, here are some guidelines for digging in to that project.

Choose an area you'd like to beautify, improve, or restore. Make sure you have permission to work in the area. You may not be allowed to work in some places because of safety issues, or because plans are already in motion to do that work.

Know what you can plant for your area. Local nurseries will usually carry only the trees, shrubs, and flowers that will grow well in your area. The people who work there know about what to plant and when to plant it. If you have the time and patience, you can research for yourself the kinds of things that grow well in your area.

Make sure you have the tools and help you will need to do your project.

Doing good work is rewarding, and working as a team can be a lot of fun too. This clean-up crew did their good work in Kansas after a tornado.

Some things take longer than you think to accomplish, so take it step by step. There is a story about a big field of daffodil flowers. When the flowers bloomed, people came from all over to see the seemingly endless view of the beautiful flowers. At the edge of the field was a sign put up by the lady who planted them. She told the visitors that she planted the bulbs over time, *one bulb at a time*. That means that little by little, you too can make an impact with the planting that you do.

Whatever you choose to plant, or if you are a helper under someone else's guidance, this is something that will continue to give for years to come.

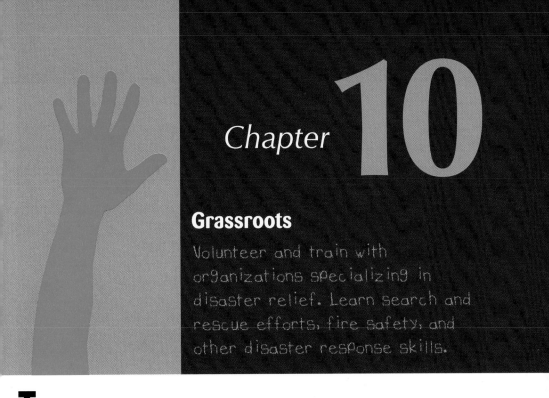

Grassroots

Volunteer and train with organizations specializing in disaster relief. Learn search and rescue efforts, fire safety, and other disaster response skills.

There are many civic organizations—groups of people who come together to make a positive difference—working to help the country build and grow. You can volunteer for one of these organizations and receive extra training for disaster relief.

CERT
Community Emergency Response Team, or CERT, is a program that educates and trains people in the community in basic skills that can be used in a disaster situation. No need to panic when you're trained to evaluate a situation and take action. Using skills taught by CERT through classroom time and exercises helps you build skills for life. Through CERT, participants learn things such as light search and rescue, fire safety, and other disaster response skills.

The age you can volunteer with a CERT program will vary depending on the community and the program. Check with your local programs, which you can find through https://www.citizencorps.gov/cert/.

Though you may be too young to officially start a CERT program in your community, you are not too young to encourage adults you know to participate in or help set up a CERT program. Another exciting option is to see if you can organize Teen CERT, which teaches skills to teens in schools. For information on how to get a Teen CERT program started in your school, start here: http://teencert.org/.

Students participate in a drill of a disaster situation as part of the CERT training in Washington, D.C. Emergency management professionals trained the team, which then gave presentations to citizens at local parks and day camps.

Citizen Corps

CERT is a program within Citizen Corps. This grassroots organization calls on American citizens to volunteer and to help in emergency situations. In a major natural disaster, it will likely take a while before official rescue efforts can bring relief to an area. If local citizens are prepared to handle emergencies, more people can be kept safe and can get the care they need. You can learn more about Citizen Corps at http://www.citizencorps.gov.

AmeriCorps

AmeriCorps has a network of partnerships with nonprofit organizations. Responding to natural disasters is one of many services that it provides. For people over 17, there are many opportunities with AmeriCorps that offer training and even the possibility of a small income while you work. Learn more at http://americorps.gov/.

Volunteering takes energy. Know in your mind and heart that all the good things you do in the world bring light and comfort. Sometimes people will be so wrapped up in their personal trauma that they will forget to say thank you. Don't worry about it, because that doesn't change the goodness you helped bring to your community.

I hope you will celebrate your successes and know that each small act can mean a world of difference. Keep up the good work, and keep your spirits high!

National Organizations
American Red Cross National Headquarters
2025 E Street, NW
Washington, DC 20006
202-303-5000
Donation Hotline: 1-800-733-2767
http://www.redcross.org

Centers for Disease Control and Prevention
1600 Clifton Road
Atlanta, GA 30333
800-CDC-INFO (1-800-232-4636)
TTY: 1-888-232-6348
http://www.cdc.gov

Community Emergency Response Team (CERT)
https://www.citizencorps.gov/cc/CertIndex.
   do?submitByState

Disaster News Network
Disaster Volunteers
c/o Village Life Company
Three Centre Park
8815 Centre Park Dr. #240
Columbia, MD 21045-2013
410-884-7350 or toll-free at 888-384-3028
http://www.disastervolunteers.org

Federal Emergency Management Agency
P.O. Box 10055
Hyattsville, MD 20782-7055
800-621-FEMA (3362)
http://www.fema.gov

National Weather Service
1325 East West Highway
Silver Spring, MD 20910
http://www.nws.noaa.gov/education.html

U.S. Geological Survey
National Center
12201 Sunrise Valley Drive
Reston, VA 20192
703-648-4000
http://www.usgs.gov

Youth Volunteer Corps of America
4600 W. 51st Street, Ste 300
Shawnee Mission, KS 66205
888-828-9822 or 913-432-9822
http://www.yvca.org

Alabama
Alabama Emergency Management Agency
P.O. Drawer 2160
5898 County Road 41
Clanton, AL 35046-2160
205-280-2200
http://ema.alabama.gov/

American Red Cross of Central Alabama
5015 Woods Crossing
Montgomery, AL 36106
334-260-3980
http://www.montgomeryarc.org/

Alaska
State of Alaska Citizen Corps Council
P.O. Box 5750
Fort Richardson, AK 99505
907-428-7000
http://www.ak-prepared.com

United Way of Anchorage
701 W. 8th Avenue, Ste 230
Anchorage, Alaska 99501
907-263-3800
http://www.liveunitedanchorage.org

Arizona
Arizona Department of Homeland Security
1700 W Washington Street, Ste 210
Phoenix, AZ 85007
602-542-7030
http://www.azdohs.gov/

Arizona Division of Emergency Management
5636 E McDowell Road
Phoenix, AZ 85008-3495
800-411-ADEM (2336) or 602-244-0504
http://www.dem.azdema.gov

Arkansas
American Red Cross Greater Arkansas
401 South Monroe
Little Rock, AR 72205
501-748-1030
http://www.redcrosslittlerock.org/

Arkansas Department of Emergency
   Management
Bldg 9501, Camp Joseph T. Robinson
North Little Rock, AR 72199
501-683-6700
http://www.adem.arkansas.gov/

California
California Emergency Management Agency
3650 Schriever Avenue
Mather, CA 95655
916-845-8510
http://www.calema.ca.gov

International Relief Teams
4560 Alvarado Canyon Road, Ste 2G
San Diego, CA 92120
619-284-7979
http://www.irteams.org

Los Angeles Regional Foodbank
1734 E. 41st Street
Los Angeles, CA 90058
323-234-3030
http://www.lafightshunger.org

Operation USA
3617 Hayden Avenue, Ste A
Culver City, CA 90232
310-838-3455
http://www.opusa.org

The Southern California Earthquake Center
http://www.scec.org/

Colorado
American Red Cross Colorado Chapters
444 Sherman Street
Denver, CO 80203-4425
303-722-7474
http://www.denver-redcross.org

Bonfils Blood Center
717 Yosemite Street
Denver, CO 80230
303-341-4000
http://www.bonfils.org

Citizens Corps in Colorado
9195 East Mineral Avenue, Ste 270
Centennial, CO 80112
720-852-6650
http://dola.colorado.gov/dem/citizen_corps/
    citizen_corps.htm

Connecticut
AmeriCares
88 Hamilton Avenue
Stamford, CT 06902
800-486-4357
http://www.americares.org/

Delaware
Delaware Emergency Management Agency
165 Brick Store Landing Road
Smyrna, DE 19977
302-659-DEMA
    or 877-SAY-DEMA (877-729-3362)—DE only
302-659-6855
http://www.dema.delaware.gov/

District of Columbia
B'nai B'rith International
2020 K Street, NW, 7th Floor
Washington, DC 20006
202-857-6600
http://www.bnaibrith.org

International Association for Human Values
2401 15th Street NW
Washington, DC 20009
202-363-2136
http://www.iahv.org

Florida
American Red Cross Mid-Florida Region
Central Florida Headquarters
5 N Bumby Avenue
Orlando, FL 32803
407-894-4141
http://www.midfloridaredcross.org

Florida Division of Emergency Management
2555 Shumard Oak Boulevard
Tallahassee, FL 32399-2100
850-413-9969
TDD/TTY: 800-226-4329
http://www.floridadisaster.org/

Georgia
Hosea Feed The Hungry: International Relief
    Fund
1035 Donnelly Avenue SW
Atlanta, GA 30310
404-755-3353
http://www.hoseafeedthehungry.com

Red Cross Atlanta
Metropolitan Atlanta Chapter
1955 Monroe Drive, NE
Atlanta, GA 30324
404-575-3730
http://www.redcrossatlanta.org

Hawaii
American Red Cross Hawaii State Chapter
    Headquarters
4155 Diamond Head Road
Honolulu, HI 96816
808-734-2101
http://www.hawaiiredcross.org

Hawaii State Civil Defense
3949 Diamond Head Road
Honolulu, HI 96816-4495
808-733-4300
TTY: 808-733-4284
http://www.scd.state.hi.us/

Idaho
The Idaho Food Bank
3562 So. T.K. Avenue
Boise, ID 83705
208-336-9643
http://www.idahofoodbank.org/

United Way of Southeastern Idaho
PO Box 911
Pocatello, ID 83204
208-232-1389
http://www.idaho.unitedway.org

Illinois
Lions Clubs International Foundation
300 West 22nd Street
Oak Brook, IL 60523
630-571-5466
http://www.lcif.org

Lutheran Disaster Response (LDR)
PO Box 71764
Chicago, IL 60694
800-638-3522, ext. 2748 or 773-380-2748
http://www.ldr.org

Indiana
Indiana Department of Homeland Security
Indiana Government Center South
302 W. Washington Street, Room E-208
Indianapolis, IN 46204
317-232-3980
http://www.in.gov/dhs

United Way of Central Indiana
3901 N. Meridian Street
P.O. Box 88409
Indianapolis, IN 46208-0409
317-923-1466
http://www.uwci.org

Iowa
United Way of Central Iowa
1111 Ninth Street, Ste 100
Des Moines, IA 50314
515-246-6500
http://www.unitedwaydm.org/

Volunteer Iowa
Iowa Commission on Volunteer Service
200 East Grand Avenue
Des Moines, IA 50309
515-242-4799
Toll-free: 800-308-5987
http://www.volunteeriowa.org

Kansas
Heart-to-Heart International, Inc.
401 S Clairborne, Ste 302
Olathe, KS 66062
913-764-5200
http://www.hearttoheart.org

Midway Kansas Red Cross
1900 East Douglas
Wichita, KS 67214
316-219-4000
http://midwaykansas.redcross.org

Youth Volunteer Corps of America
4600 W. 51st Street, Ste 300
Shawnee Mission, KS 66205
888-828-9822 or 913-432-9822
http://www.yvca.org

Kentucky
Kentucky Division of Emergency Management
Emergency Management
100 Minuteman Parkway
Frankfort, KY 40601
502-607-1611
http://kyem.ky.gov

United Way of Kentucky
P.O. Box 4653
Louisville, KY 40204
502-589-6897
http://www.uwky.org

Louisiana
Southeast Louisiana Red Cross
Robert W. Merrick Building
2640 Canal Street
New Orleans, LA 70119504-620-3105
http://www.arcno.org

Volunteers of America: Greater New Orleans
127 S. Solomon Street
New Orleans, LA 70119
504-483-3557
504-333-6395
www.voagno.org

Maine
American Red Cross of Southern Maine
2401 Congress Street
Portland, ME 04102
207-874-1192
207-795-4004
Toll Free: 877-372-7363
http://southernmaine.redcross.org/

Maine Emergency Management Agency
72 State House Station
45 Commerce Dr.
Augusta, ME 04333
800-452-8735 (in-state only)
207-624-4400
TTY: 877-789-0200 / 207-629-5793
http://www.maine.gov/MEMA

Maryland
Ananda Marga Universal Relief Team (AMURT)
2502 Lindley Terrace
Rockville, MD 20850
http://www.amurt.net

Baltimore County Volunteers
611 Central Avenue, Rm. 314
Towson, MD 21204
410-887-2736
http://www.baltimorecountymd.gov/
   Agencies/volunteers

Maryland Volunteers
Find volunteer opportunities in your county.
http://www.marylandvolunteercenters.org/

Massachusetts
Massachusetts Office of Coastal Zone
   Management: Hurricane Preparedness
251 Causeway Street, Ste 800
Boston, MA 02114-2138
617-626-1200
http://www.mass.gov/czm/hurricanes.htm

United Way of Massachusetts Bay and
   Merrimack Valley
51 Sleeper Street
Boston, MA 02210
617-624-8000
http://supportunitedway.org/

Michigan
Michigan Citizen Corps
4000 Collins Road
Lansing, MI 48910
517-336-6429
http://tinyurl.com/5un7q

Michigan Prepares
http://www.michigan.gov/michiganprepares

Volunteers of America Michigan
21415 Civic Center Drive, Ste 210
Southfield, MI 48076
248-945-0101
http://www.voami.org/

Minnesota
Greater Twin Cities United Way
404 South Eighth Street
Minneapolis, MN 55404-1084
612-340-7400
http://www.unitedwaytwincities.org

Minnesota Citizen Corps Council
MN Homeland Security and Emergency Mgt.
444 Cedar Street, Ste 223
St. Paul, MN 55101-6223
651-201-7442
http://www.hsem.state.mn.us

Mississippi
Central Mississippi Chapter, American Red
   Cross
875 Riverside Drive
Jackson, MS 39211
601-353-5442
http://www.mississippi-redcross.org/

Mississippi Commission for Volunteer Service
3825 Ridgewood Road, Ste 601
Jackson, MS 39211
601-432-6779
Toll Free: 888-353-1793
http://www.mcvs.org/

Missouri
Convoy of Hope
330 S Patterson Avenue
Springfield, MO 65802
417-823-8998
http://www.convoyofhope.org/

National Council of the United States
Society of St. Vincent de Paul
58 Progress Parkway
St. Louis, MO 63043
314-576-3993
http://www.svdpusa.org

Montana
American Red Cross of Montana
1300 28th Street S., 3rd Floor
Great Falls, MT 59405
800-ARC-MONT
http://www.montanaredcross.org/

United Way of Lewis & Clark County
75 East Lyndale, P.O. Box 862
Helena, Montana 59624
406-442-4360
http://www.uwlcc.com/

Nebraska
American Red Cross, Northeast Nebraska
   Chapter
106 West 3rd Street, P.O. Box 94
Wayne, NE 68787
402-375-5209
http://www.northeastnebraskaredcross.org/

Serve Nebraska
P.O. Box 98927
Lincoln, NE 68509-8927
800-291-8911
http://serve.nebraska.gov/

Nevada
Northern Nevada Chapter, American Red
   Cross
1190 Corporate Boulevard
Reno, NV 89502
775-856-1000
http://www.nevada.redcross.org/

State of Nevada Citizen Corps Council
500 Casino Center Boulevard
Las Vegas, NV 89101
702-229-0067
http://homelandsecurity.nv.gov

New Hampshire
Granite Chapter American Red Cross
2 Maitland Street
Concord, NH 03301
800-464-6692
http://www.concord-redcross.org

Volunteer New Hampshire
603-271-7200
http://www.volunteernh.org

New Jersey
Pass It Along
60 Blue Heron Road, Ste 100
Sparta, NJ 07871
973-726-9777
http://www.passitalong.org

The Volunteer Network
513 W. Mt. Pleasant Avenue
Livingston, NJ 07039
973-740-0588
http://www.volunteernj.org/

Volunteer New Jersey
http://www.volunteernewjersey.org/vnj/

New Mexico
New Mexico Commission for Community
   Volunteerism
3401 Pan American Freeway, NE
Albuquerque, NM 87107
505-841-4811
http://www.newmexserve.org

Southwestern New Mexico Red Cross
1301 E Griggs
Las Cruces, NM 88001
575-526-2631
http://www.swnmredcross.org/

New York
New York State Citizen Corps Council
New York State Emergency Management
   Office
1220 Washington Avenue, Ste 101, Bldg 22
Albany, NY 12226
518-292-2326
http://www.semo.state.ny.us

New York State Commission on National &
   Community Service
52 Washington St
North Building—Suite 338
Rensselaer, NY 12144
518-473-8882
http://www.newyorkersvolunteer.ny.gov/
   DisasterPreparedness/Overview.aspx

North Carolina
American Red Cross Triangle Area Chapter
100 North Peartree Lane
Raleigh, NC 27610
919-231-1602

507 N Steele Street # H212
Sanford, NC 27330
919-774-6857

801 S 3rd Street
Smithfield, NC 27577
919-934-8481

http://www.trianglearc.org/

Hearts With Hands Inc.
951 Sand Hill Road
Asheville, NC 28806
828-667-1912 or 800-726-9185
http://www.heartswithhands.org

North Dakota
United Way of Cass-Clay
219 7th Street S
Fargo, ND 58103
701-237-5050
http://www.uwcc.net/

Ohio
American Red Cross of Greater Columbus
995 E. Broad Street
Columbus, OH 43205
614-253-2740
http://columbus.redcross.org

Delaware County Red Cross
380 Hills-Miller Road
Delaware, OH 43015
740-362-2021
http://www.delco-redcross.org/

Serve Ohio
51 N. High Street, Ste 800
Columbus, OH 43215
Ohio Community Service Council
   (OCSC): 614-728-2916
CNCS State Office: 614-469-7441
http://www.serveohio.org/

Oklahoma
American Red Cross of Central Oklahoma
601 NE 6th Street
Oklahoma City, OK 73104
405-228-9500
http://okc.redcross.org/

Oklahoma Department of Emergency
    Management
2401 Lincoln Boulevard—Ste C51
Oklahoma City, OK 73105
405-521-2481
http://www.ok.gov/OEM/

Oregon
Oregon Red Cross
3131 N. Vancouver Avenue
Portland, OR 97227
503-284-1234
http://www.oregonredcross.org/

United Way of Lane County
3171 Gateway Loop
Springfield, OR 97477
541-741-6000
http://www.unitedwaylane.org/

Pennsylvania
American Red Cross
Southeastern Pennsylvania: Disaster Services
215-299-4889 (24 hours a day)
Blood Services
215-451-4000 or (800) GIVE-LIFE
Youth Services & Instructor Inquiries
215-299-4027
http://www.redcrossphilly.org

Mennonite Disaster Service (MDS)
1018 Main Street
Akron, PA 17501
717-859-2210
http://www.mds.mennonite.net

Rhode Island
Serve Rhode Island
655 Broad Street
Providence, RI 02907
401-331-2298
http://serverhodeisland.org

United Way of Rhode Island
50 Valley Street
Providence, RI 02909-2459
401-444-0600
http://www.uwri.org

Volunteer Center:
http://www.vcri.org/matriarch/default.asp

South Carolina
Coastal South Carolina Chapter of the
    American Red Cross
2795 Pampas Drive
Myrtle Beach, SC 29577
843-477-0020
http://horrycounty.redcross.org/

South Carolina Emergency Management Div
2779 Fish Hatchery Road
West Columbia, SC 29172
803-737-8500
http://www.scemd.org

South Dakota
American Red Cross, Sioux Empire Chapter
808 N. West Avenue
Sioux Falls, SD 57104
605-336-2448
http://www.siouxempireredcross.org/

South Dakota Department of Public
    Safety: Emergency Services: Emergency
    Management
118 W. Capitol Avenue
Pierre, SD 57501
605-773-3231
605-773-3178
http://dps.sd.gov/emergency_services/
    emergency_management/default.aspx

Tennessee
Memphis/Shelby County Emergency
    Management Agency
2668 Avery
Memphis, TN 38112-4812
901-515-2525, ext. 2601
http://www.mscema.org

Red Cross Heart of Tennessee Chapter
836 Commercial Court
Murfreesboro, TN 37129
615-893-4272
http://www.midtnredcross.org/

United Way of Tennessee
209 Gothic Court, Ste 107
Franklin, TN 37067
615-791-1464
http://www.uwtn.org/

Texas
Reach Out America International Inc.
9901 Windmill Lakes
Houston, TX 77275
281-857-1234
http://www.reachoutamerica.org/

Red Cross Dallas
4800 Harry Hines Boulevard
Dallas, TX 75235-7717
214-678-4800
http://www.redcrossdallas.org

Texas Episcopal Disaster Relief
1225 Texas Avenue
Houston, TX 77002
800-318-4452 or 713-520-6444
http://www.epicenter.org/

Texas State Citizen Corps Council
Texas Association of Regional Councils
701 Brazos, Ste 780
Austin, TX 78701
512-275-9308
http://www.texascitizencorps.org/

Utah
Association of Volunteer Emergency Response
   Teams
AVERT USA
P. O. Box 27222
Salt Lake City, Utah 84127-0222
801-468-2779
http://www.avertdisasters.org

United Way of Salt Lake
175 S. West Temple, Ste 30
Salt Lake City, UT 84101-1424
801-736-8929
http://www.uw.org/

Vermont
American Red Cross Vermont and the New
   Hampshire Valley
29 Mansfield Avenue
Burlington, VT 05401-3323
802-660-9130
http://vermontredcross.org/
http://www.redcrossvtnhuv.org

United Way of Chittenden County
412 Farrell Street, Ste 200
South Burlington, VT 05403
802-864-7541 or 800-545-0446
http://www.unitedwaycc.org

Virginia
Project HOPE—The People-to-People Health
   Foundation, Inc.
255 Carter Hall Lane
Millwood, VA 22646
800-544-4673
http://www.projecthope.org

Virginia Department of Emergency
   Management
10501 Trade Court
Richmond, VA 23236
804-674-2400
http://www.vdem.state.va.us/citcorps/
   index.cfm

Washington
Seattle Red Cross
900 25th Avenue South, P.O. Box 3097
Seattle, WA 98114
206-323-2345

811 Pacific Avenue, P.O. Box 499
Bremerton, WA 98337
360-377-3761
http://www.seattleredcross.org/

United Way of King County Offices
720 Second Avenue
Seattle, WA 981042
206-461-3700
http://www.uwkc.org

Washington Voluntary Organizations Active in
   Disaster
http://wavoad.org/

West Virginia
United Way of Central West Virginia
One United Way Square
Charleston, WV 25301
304-340-3500
http://www.unitedwaycwv.org

West Virginia Division of Homeland Security
   and Emergency Management
Bldg. 1, Rm. EB-80
1900 Kanawha Boulevard
East Charleston, WV 25305
304-558-5380
http://www.wvdhsem.gov/

Wisconsin
American Red Cross Chapters Active in
   Wisconsin
http://www.wi-redcross.org/

American Red Cross Northwest Wisconsin
3057 Michigan Avenue
Stevens Point, WI 54481
715-344-4052
http://www.redcrossncwi.com

United Way Wisconsin
2059 Atwood Avenue
Madison, WI 53704
608-246-8272
http://www.unitedwaywi.org

Wyoming
American Red Cross of Wyoming
3619 Evans Avenue, P.O. Box 586
Cheyenne, WY 82003
307-638-8906
http://www.wyomingredcross.org/

United Way of Southwest Wyoming
404 N Street, Ste 301
Rock Springs, WY 82901
307-362-5003
http://www.swunitedway.org

Further Reading

On the Internet
FEMA for Kids: http://www.fema.gov/kids/
Kids Are Heroes: http://www.kidsareheroes.com

Works Consulted
Center for International Disaster Information (CIDI): http://www.cidi.org/guidelines/guide_ln.htm
FEMA. *Are You Ready? A Guide For Citizen Preparedness.* August 2004. http://www.fema.gov/areyouready/
FEMA: http://www.fema.gov/
"Flight 232: Snapshots of Tragedy and Triumph." http://www.ktiv.com/global/story.asp?s=10747976
Goode, Caron B., Tom Goode, and David Russell. *Help Kids Cope with Stress and Trauma.* Ft Worth, TX: Inspired Living International, 2006.
KidsHealth: http://kidshealth.org/
Kilroy, Chris. "Special Report: United Airlines Flight 232." http://www.airdisaster.com/special/special-ua232.shtml
Ready.gov (disaster preparedness tips from FEMA): http://www.ready.gov/
Red Cross: http://www.redcross.org/
Waldman, Jackie. *Teens with the Courage to Give: Young People Who Triumphed Over Tragedy and Volunteered to Make a Difference.* Berkeley, CA: Conari Press, 2000.

Chapter 1. Teaching Preparedness
FEMA: http://www.fema.gov/plan/prepare/basickit.shtm
NOAA: http://www.nhc.noaa.gov/HAW2/english/prepare/supply_kit.shtml
Ready America (Get A Kit): http://www.ready.gov/america/getakit/
Red Cross: http://tinyurl.com/l4cjg5

SFGate: http://www.sfgate.com/cgi-bin/article.cgi?f=/earthquakes/archive/ready.dtl
USA Evacuation Routes: http://www.ibiblio.org/rcip/evacuationroutes.html

Chapter 2. Connecting in an Emergency
Blenthien, Mark. "After an Earthquake": http://www.videojug.com/interview/staying-safe-after-an-earthquake
Emergency Alert System: http://www.fcc.gov/pshs/services/eas/
FEMA: Plan Ahead: http://www.fema.gov/plan/index.shtm
FEMA: What to Do in a Flood: http://www.fema.gov/hazard/flood/fl_during.shtm
FEMA: What to Do in a Tornado: http://www.fema.gov/hazard/tornado/to_during.shtm
Fire Safety: http://www.firesafety.gov/
Integrated Public Alert and Warning System (IPAWS): http://www.fema.gov/emergency/ipaws/
Kids Health: http://kidshealth.org/parent/firstaid_safe/emergencies/help.html
NOAA: http://www.nws.noaa.gov/nwr/ list of stations you can tune in for weather info
Ready.Gov: http://www.ready.gov/kids/step2/index.html

Chapter 3. Volunteer Your Time or Skills
Animals: http://animals.com/collection/Volunteer
Disaster Prepped: http://www.disasterprepped.com/cleanup.php
OSHA: http://www.osha.gov/OshDoc/cleanupHazard.html
Ready.gov (animal preparedness) http://www.ready.gov/america/getakit/pets.html

Further Reading

UMN: http://www.extension.umn.edu/
administrative/disasterresponse/
disaster.html
Volunteer Work with Animals:
http://hubpages.com/hub/
Volunteer-Work-with-Animals

Chapter 4. Giving Emotional Support to Other Kids
Family Guide: http://family.samhsa.
gov/talk/destress.aspx
FEMA. Becoming a Disaster Action Kid:
http://www.fema.gov/kids/dizkid1.
htm
Helping Children After a Natural
Disaster: http://www.nasponline.
org/resources/crisis_safety/
naturaldisaster_ho.aspx

Chapter 5. Organizing Child Care While Adults Rebuild
Babysitting Tips: http://www.
babysittingtips.net/
Games Kids Play: http://www.
gameskidsplay.net/
"Six Rules for Babysitting": http://
kidsactivities.suite101.com/article.
cfm/rules_for_babysitting

Chapter 6. Blood Drive
Bonfils Blood Center: http://www.
bonfils.org/
Red Cross: http://www.givelife2.org/
donor/top10.asp
Red Cross: http://www.givelife2.org/
sponsor/checklist.asp

Chapter 7. Food and Clothing Drives
Charity Guide: http://www.
charityguide.org/volunteer/fifteen/
clothesshoes.htm

Feeding America: http://
feedingamerica.org
Give Spot: http://www.givespot.com/
donate/food.htm
Goodwill Industries International:
http://www.goodwill.org/
Lions Club International
http://www.lionsclub.org/
Planet Aid: http://www.planetaid.org/
Salvation Army: http://www.
salvationarmyusa.org

Chapter 8. Fund-raising for Charities
American Red Cross: http://www.
redcross.org/
Charity Watch: http://www.
charitywatch.org/toprated.html
Children Incorporated: http://www.
children-inc.org
Food for the Hungry: http://www.
fh.org/
Gifts in Kind: http://www.giftsinkind.
org/
Save the Children: http://www.
savethechildren.org

Chapter 9. Replanting
Trees Forever: http://www.treesforever.
org/
U.S. Forest Service: http://www.fs.fed.
us/

Chapter 10. Grassroots
AmeriCorps: http://americorps.gov/
Citizen Corps: http://citizencorps.gov/
Citizen Emergency Response Teams
(CERT): https://www.citizencorps.
gov/cert/

Index

911 (emergency number) 12, 15

American Red Cross 7, 15, 25, 27

AmeriCorps 37

basic supply kit (list) 9

blood drive 24–25

breathing to relax 20

call centers 15

child care 18, 21–23
  art projects 21
  food 22
  games 22
  singing 18, 20
  storytelling 22

Citizen Corps 37

cleanup 15–16

clothing drive 26–28

Community Emergency Response Team (CERT) 35–36, 37

Emergency Alert System (EAS) 14

evacuation 8, 10, 14

family preparedness plan 13

fear, techniques to ease 18–20

FEMA (Federal Emergency Management Agency) 4, 7

fire safety 13

first response 14

flyers 11, 27–28

food drive 26–28

fund-raising 29–32
  bake sale 32
  donation tables 30
  lemonade stands 30
  running/swimming laps 30, 31

Integrated Public Alert and Warning System (IPAWS) 14

Lions Club 27

natural disasters
  blizzards 4, 7, 8
  earthquakes 4, 7–8, 13
  flooding 4, 6, 14, 15
  human-caused disasters 4, 24
  hurricanes 4, 13, 14, 17, 30, 31
  mudslides 4, 33
  tornadoes 13, 15, 34
  tsunamis 32
  wildfires 4

online networking 13

parental permission 5

pet care 9, 16–17

phone list 10, 11, 12, 13

planting 33–34

positive self-talk 20

preparedness 6, 7–10, 11, 12, 13

preparedness kit 7–8, 9, 10, 11–14

radio 9, 14, 28

Salvation Army 27

Save the Children 29

seniors 16

shelters 14, 15

Society for the Prevention of Cruelty to Animals (SPCA) 17

training 35–37

volunteer 15–17, 35, 37

Laya Saul has been involved with community service from a young age, from teaching first aid and CPR for the Red Cross to volunteering with youth and starting community organizations that will serve and educate their members. She has been involved with various charities and has seen firsthand the good that can come from donating time and money to worthy causes.

Laya is also known to lots of people as Aunt Laya because she wrote a book for teens (called *You Don't Have to Learn Everything the Hard Way*) to help them live happier, safer lives.

Born in Los Angeles, California, she now lives gratefully with her husband, kids, dog, and cat in Israel.

Laya believes that with constant small acts of love or kindness to each other we can bring about a peaceful world, just like lighting one small candle will chase away the darkness.